THE JOURNEY

"SHE LIVED WHILE SHE LOVED"

MANOUSHIKHA PURKAYASTHA

Dedication

Writing for me is like connecting to all. It gives the strength to my inner core to keep up going. My heartiest dedications to you and you motivations which enabled me to reach up to here.
You has always taught me to fight with every situation with a positive attitude and keep patience when anything is not working well because we have no control over the situations but we can control ourselves. Thanks always for being such a lovely part of my life and keep me going in my worst days too.

Contents

Foreword

The Journey (She Lived while She Loved) contains some deep down thoughts of the author which one faces while being in love with someone very close. The author has tried her best to incorporate all her emotions to words so that you all can understand the real meaning and the ethics of unconditional love. She wants you all to follow such a path in which there's no place for revenge or give and take formalities of true love. The author writes about someone who's going through a phase in which she has loved deeply and lived the moments of utmost silence. The author tried to make you understand the worth of patience to save many things rather than revolting back.

She wants you to realise that patience has an utmost power. She's looking forward to all your praises and critics and wishes that her words may be imprinted in your hearts forever.

Preface

The Journey (She Lived while She Loved) is not just a book for me. It's my heart core feelings and emotions which I've tried to pen down in one platform. The book comprises of quotes and poetries based on my own thoughts and feelings. It's a compilation of all the thoughts one have and the situations one faces when "BEING IN LOVE" with someone....... Focus on the words "Being in Love" not just "Being in a Relationship". The book focuses on such a journey of a person who has loved eternally and wants to be loved a lot as she's tired now of being strong forever and wants someone to understand her unsaid words.
It tells us about that always the things does not go as per our expectations but then also we need to keep patience as we can't control the situations but we can control ourselves. In such an era of fake ideas and faces, the book gives an idea of how one can "Love Unconditionally" and what are the situations one go through in the process. I believe Love is such an emotion which is does not depend what you feel. Rather it depends on the fact that what the other person is feeling and going through.

I've tried to make you all understand through my words that pure and true love is not based on situations and cannot be parted by distance. Whatsoever the circumstances are, but one's love can never be changed once truly imprinted in the heart. It lasts forever. One should have the courage to stand by your closed ones when your feelings are true. Mere promises doesn't work, you need to practice as well. There's nothing which can happen but cannot be continued further if there's a strong will. Hope you all will love my thoughts and will try to understand the meaning of selfless and unconditional love.

Acknowledgements

I feel really blessed to be capable of expressing my thoughts and views through my words. Really thankful to God who made me write all my feelings in words and gave me the extreme level of patience to stand by my closed ones.
Special thanks to my too special one who has always motivated me to grow further in my life and made me see life with a new perspective.

I'm grateful to all my friends who always gave me constant support to write further and better and better. They always praise all my writings and also help me to reform in a better way every time and also point out my mistakes to come out as a different me.

I really pray to God that my views on unconditional love never changes and May I follow the path of eternal and selfless emotions which I want you all to move upon.

1. "So, Here we are......."

- *When I see your name in the notification, a spark lits up in my core wishing to have you in my arms asap......*

- *Nothing stays the same after once the strings of heart gets detached.......*

- *You're like a lamp, who lits me up with your care and love whenever I'm in dark woods of grief.......*

- *If I know what love is, it's because of the feeling I've felt having your Love........*

- *'I could never forget you'*
  'But why?'
  'Because your name beats with my heartbeat.........'

• *All my roads needs to a single destination.....That is....."YOU".....*

• *It's not easy to have patience*
BUT
It's essence of purity is worth......

• *Love taught me the worth of waiting and then getting the essence of purity.......*

• *Whenever I feel stressed seeing the upcoming problems towards me,*
I end up thinking by realising that you're there to handle everything and take me out of every situation.......

• *When the night gets darker, the feeling emerges from the corner of eyes in the form of pearl of tears.......*

• *When you really fall for someone whatsoever the situation is ....Your heart becomes calm with their single contact.......*

• *I feel truly happy when your hands are entangled with mine,*
It feels me with a new joy and a new shine.......

• *Love without communication is like a flower without aesthetics.......*

• *To the moonlight that is visiting me tonight,*
Let my beloved know of my love by showering your light,
You're the connector between me and my Mr. Right
You're the witness of all our lovely memories with love and full of fights.......

• *Love finds you*
When you are at your worst......

• *If my heart could speak, it'd say*
it just needs your warmth to beat forever and ever.........

• *Love stories often begin with unexpected meetings.......*

• *Those who truly love you will never leave you even in the toughest situation*
Because they'll always try to find out solutions to fight those with you not without you........

• *In love it hurts, when the person you love changes with time......*

• *Freedom to me is when I can express all my views in front of you......*

• *I understood the meaning of love when the cloud of tears appeared in my eyes just mere talking about getting detached from you.......*

• *A book is a dream that contains a lot full of expectations, emotions and memories.......*

• *My heart is scared of losing your heart beat......*

• *Some people are like sweaters who protect you from the outer world's cold of problems.......*

• *Sunflowers taught me to show my brightest side to the world hiding the darker and hurted side of my heart in my core........*

• *I still find love in my every bit of soul.........*

• *When the sun rays touch my face*
I get a new glow of strength and it reminds me of our dreams together.......

• *Mornings are meant for a new start and gives me a strength to start afresh in every situation with you and holding your hand throughout.......*

• *The flowers in my garden tell me that I'm also a queen flower of someone else' garden......*

• *Problems taught me that they last only until you don't stop getting bothered by them.......*

• I found my home in you and only you........

• When I share my secrets with the moon,
It asks, where the person has gone who is the reason for all......

• Memory is that receipt which ensures the attachment and gives the assurance of connection.......

• When I think a lot then I realise that you do it all just for my happiness.... It's just that your path chosen is a bit different.......

• I lose myself
Only when
I lose you.......

• My heart is a refrigerator and you are the sweets which enhances it's beauty........

• When love visits,
It knocks on that darkest part of our heart which has never seen the glimpse and shade of outer world and enhances it to a new individual.........

• As I looked in the mirror, a reflection of you in me......

• Sometimes, we only need someone
Who just says......Yes you proceed......I'm there with you no matter what.......

• One word that gives me strength and confidence is .....''WE''.....
Whenever you start any conversation and denotes us as we, I can feel the warmth of our bonding which gives me an inspirationto start afresh.......

• The biggest lie I've ever told is....
I don't want you.....

• *The most selfish thing I've ever done is I prayed for you to be happy so that I can be happy by seeing your happiness.......*

• *The old me loved you and always wants to see you,*
The new me loves you but is satisfied with the distance........

• *Loneliness appeared I came to know you are away and not mine,*
Loneliness disappeared when I realised we all came alone in this world and there's nothing our own here.......

• *I feel amazing about myself when*
I realise all my efforts with due patience for you irrespective of all the ignorance I received........

• *Reading you is like going through deeper and deeper in the sea of love, care, knowledge and awful nature of yours........*

• Love is not an event
But it is the whole year....suggesting that it is permanent not just momentary.........

• Love is not a solution to end problems
But it is a key to a path which helps to handle them with patience.........

• The most wonderful day in my life was when I realised that .....yes it's only you and you're the one........

• Your eyes are like stars which enlighten my dark sky of life with it's glaze.......

• There's nothing like healing......It's just that we start accepting the situations and reality and they hurt less after a period of time ....Healing is when you don't get hurt at all remembering the old times.......And it is not possible because if your feelings are true then it is itself permanent and with every feeling there's a lot full of memories attached which are connected to a flow of emotions so every single time when we recall that time it fills our heart with the same feelings we had earlier and hurts ....so in short it hurts less but not completely zero.......And therefore no healing has occurred it's just

that we have gained a control on our heart and mind over a period of time........

• *I've moved on but....*
with your memories and towards a new life with an aim of accomplishing our dream which we dreamt together........

• *"Why would you not say yes to me?" He asked...*
"There's no formalities of permission in our relationship...."
I replied........

• *I can't get over the fact that*
I'm yours......

• *I like to hold*
Your every darkness with a tight grip along with your glaze..........

• I feel stressed when you are far away from me
AND
I feel relaxed when you hold my hand and say "No worries......I'm there with you no matter what.....irrespective of the distance........"

• My life took an unpredictable turn when you turned away from me.........

• When I first met you
I was unaware with the start of such a beautiful part of my life.........

• When I asked you whether you will be with me forever,
You replied you are already inside me in my soul.........

• Life took me by surprise when after getting hurt everytime, I still kept patience and continued loving you.........

• The sun looks like it had burnt a lot in the past in order to get this glaze........

• You promised me that you will not break your promise.........

• Life surprised me when
It showered enormous amount of rejoice and happiness by giving me you as the sweetest gift ever...........

• Love is like a blanket
It comforts us on our cold and harsh days of our lives.........

• My life changed when
You arrived,
But I've changed when you left me alone..........

• Return to me like
The sun arrives after every phase of darkness.........

• It's not easy to write about the untold pain.......

• It's been a long time
I've made any complaints to you.......

• *All that a human truly needs is*
Love and care,
But one ends up wanting
To fulfill selfish desires.....

• *Just like you*
These stars look at me with a glaze in their eyes........

• *"No one can replace you"*
Not because "There's no one like you"
It's just because "They are not you".........

• *She was unaware that he had touched and kissed her scars and flaws not because he wants to accept her fully but in actual to scratch them further and make a new one.........*

• *The world seems smaller when I compare it with you as my whole world only surrounds you and the rest seems negligible.........*

• What hurts the most
Is your unwillingness to make any efforts..........

• If we forgive then it depicts that it is love.......
But if we forget then it indicates that it was just a relationship........

• I will find you where purity lies.......

• Being by the sea feels like engulfing into the deepness of love and peace where everything is just still and calm..........

• The future depends on your present efforts and what you sow today.......

• Before you
Came into my life, I was surviving,
After you
Arrived, I started living......

• Life has shown me there's never an end.......

• Before sunset,
I always wish to hear your voice to ensure that the end of the day is beautiful.........

• In the beginning,
We both were unaware of this wonderful and awemaking experience awaiting for us in the future............

• Even in your absence
Both the mind and the heart are busy with the your thoughts........

• When I first heard your voice,
I was unaware that one day this will be healing for me in this world full hardships...........

• Love is that person
Who always stays by your side if it's true and keeps you backing up on your back and says no matter how difficult is the situation he'll stay with you unconditionally..........

• Every word and action from your side
Gives me immense strength and infinite feelings.......

• Together, we can cover up miles of toughest paths ever........

• I'm not afraid of walking in the darkest paths but I'm scared to walk without you.........

• When you finally opened up
I realised that I've got my soulmate........

• You're like tea
Who warms me up with a new spirit even at my coldest and lowest points.........

• Sunrise is always
An indicator that every darkness of our lives will definitely have it's end........

• Before you arrived,
My life did not have any route to achieve my dreams but now you gave me a beautiful path towards our dreams

together.........

• This morning feels different
As after a long time it had started with your essence..........

• Before,
I met you, everything was turning around me like I am stuck in between but
Now,
After your arrival, I feel safe even in the toughest storms...........

• Sometimes, life gifts us something so much special unexpectedly and in such a way that when it actually comes you are really unaware of it's essence...........

• When I meet you after a long time,
I always notice your eyes and try to figure out any change but each time I can feel the heavenly experience of the same love as it was when the first time we met..........

• I felt brave when
I single handedly handled both of us from the storm of misunderstandings, distrust and developed a new flower

of love and honesty between us.........

• I waited for you like a traveller waits for a river of fresh water to arrive in the desserts........

• You're like the sky
With endless love and limitless space of faith.........

• There's not enough ink to express the story of the darkest part ever of my life.........

• It's only at night when someone in actual realises about the loneliness of their lives........

• When you are with me, I feel as if I can win the toughest war ever........

• Come, sit by my side,
Let's talk something real.....Closer to accomplishings and miles far away from mere promises.........

• *Your voice sounds like a melodious song in this world full of noise.........*

• *When something arrives after a long wait,*
It is really of much worth than the one which is freely available.........

• *Everything I do is*
Linked with you as my heart and my feelings are merged with you..........

• *When I'm alone*
I think of the memories you spent with me and
When I'm with people
I think of the memories we spent with together..........

• *Travelling with you is like*
Exploring a new me........

• *When you love*
You try to forget the whole world to give all your efforts to notice each and everything of that person but

When you leave
You try to forget all the efforts you've done and get engaged to the whole world so that you can't notice anything of that person.........

• *My world is made up of*
You, me and our dreams full of melodies and joy together holding hands and supporting each other's back forever..........

• *When you left*
My soul lost its power.......

• *Life showed me everything depends on your efforts.....*

• *Achievement isn't about having you in my life without any adversities....... It's all about having each other's love and to achieve our goals to be together forever inspite of having all adverse situations..........*

• When we meet I will tell you
How I've waited for you so long and how hard it was and will also tell you about my each and every moment in your absence........

• Togetherness is all about
Understanding each other's pain and sufferings and stand by their side no matter what and shower strength with the warmth of love to each other to face the adversities........

• Whatever I wish to say,
I always pen it down on paper as I think may be you'll not be able to bear it........

• I never wanted to leave but for me your happiness and contentment is my only priority..........

• I look at you like a thirsty person looks at a glass of water with all full of hope and satisfaction..........

• Of course
I Love You
But
I don't wanna say it loud and make you realise every time

as love never requires outer coverings. It can only be felt by the warmth of our hearts..........

• Come to me like
The morning breeze, as if the evening shines and the night sparkles........

• When you're into someone,
You start feeling them inside yourself........

• I don't ever get tired
When the miles are covered up holding your hands and having you besides.......

• I saw hope
When I heard my name echoed from your voice.......

• Holding your hands is like
Handing over all my problems and pain to you and taking over the medications to heal from the adversities.......

• The most interesting story from my life is how we met each other like strangers and reached upto eternity........

• To cheat and hurt is their choice....... To keep loving them inspite of getting hurt so much is my love and responsibility.....

• You broke my heart like
An axe having a wooden part below breaks the wood of the tree trunks inspite of being made with it's material only.........

• Talking to you is like
Applying medicines on all my painful griefs.......

• I would have left a long time ago
If I haven't loved you from my core.......

• When the moon is absent
A storm of the fear of losing you and getting parted comes in my heart and I starts feeling the distance between us........

*• Of all the things I have written
I come out with a conclusion that they all have one thing in common that is..... Your essence......and purity of our eternal love.........*

*• Night arrival is like
The reminder of all the flashbacks that had been spent just with you.......*

*• When I'm with you
I can feel the heavenly experiences..........*

*• The world feels our own when
Your most loved ones stand by you and encloses you in their arms and prevents you from all the hardships.........*

• Your departure was like my soul has departed from my body.......

*• An absence of your notification
Seems like absence of my soul which makes me feel emptiest ever........*

• When someone asks me still I love him,
I reply,
I don't love him, instead I love myself in the course of
loving him as we are not two..... United.....

• I miss you like the ripples of sea water misses the sea
shore........

• When I look at the stars,
They stand there for keeping a watch and taking care of me
in your absence......

• Looking at the rain falling through the window,
I always miss those days of our newly sprinkled love.......

• Of course
I will love you for the rest of my whole life,
But
I also want you by my side......

• You arrived in my life like the moonlight in the night
full of darkness all around.......

• Once upon a time,
We used to talk for almost the whole day....
Now,
We rarely talk in some days.....

• Before we met,
The world seemed a puzzle full of hardships to me....
After we met,
You unlocked every hardships with the key of your love.......

• The night carries me to
The darkness of my griefs and the world which makes me realise that you are really far.......

• Mondays are good when
You are there to motivate me for the whole new week.......

• If you want
To see me every morning besides you and waking you up then work for it and take a stand....
Or else,
Just accept what's happening around........

• It is never too late to express your feelings........

• Mind says
Move on he doesn't love you......
Heart says
Hold on you love him.......

• The sun wakes me up and tells me
To wait for the sunrise of happiness after a darkness of griefs in life.........

Endnote

I hope you all have loved the contents. Really eagerly waiting for your praises and critics. I just wanted that you all can feel the purity of unconditional love. Sometimes patience gives the key to all locks of problems. So have patience.

Always remember your single decision can affect anyone's whole life and you'll always be remembered by your deeds not by your name or designations etc. Also, make sure you understand what your closed ones wants from you and sometimes they also need to be loved after loving so hardly.

9 798887 839073

Printed by Libri Plureos GmbH in Hamburg,
Germany